HAIR

Written and Illustrated by
Racquel Peters

©Copyright 2022 Racquel Peters
All rights reserved. This book is protected under the copyright laws of the United States of America.
ISBN-13: 978-1-954609-40-2

No portion of this book may be reproduced, distributed, or transmitted in any form, including photocopying, recording, or other electronic or mechanical methods, without the written permission of the publisher, except in the case of brief quotations embodied in reviews and certain other non-commercial uses permitted by copyright law. Permission granted on request.

For information regarding special discounts for bulk purchases contact the Publisher:
LaBoo Publishing Enterprise, LLC
staff@laboopublishing.com
www.laboopublishing.com

I love to dance,

play outside,

and go swimming too.

I get all sweaty when I play in the mud, but I really don't care.

The only thing I have to think about is my hair.

It's shiny and straight, just how I like, but it gets frizzy with one drop of water...

and gives Mom a fright.

A bun,

puff balls,

a ponytail,

My favorite hairstyle takes time, and I have to sit and wait.

But at the end of the day, my hair looks pretty and straight.

like dance,

and go swimming too.

Why is my hair different?

Why is my hair loud?

Why do I stick out in a crowd?

Made in the USA
Columbia, SC
02 June 2024